Big thanks to Clare and Pauliina
D.W.

Fizz the shy fire engine

Scoop the boastful digger

Chug the helpful tractor

Choo the forgetful train

ORCHARD BOOKS
338 Euston Road, London NW1 3BH
Orchard Books Australia
Level 17/207 Kent Street, Sydney, NSW 2000
First published in 2003 by Orchard Books
First published in paperback in 2004
This paperback edition published in 2010
Text and illustrations © David Wojtowycz 2003
The right of David Wojtowycz to be identified as the author and illustrator of this work
has been asserted by him in accordance with the Copyright, Designs and Patents Act, 1988.
A CIP catalogue record for this book is available from the British Library.
ISBN 978 1 40830 876 9
1 3 5 7 9 10 8 6 4 2
Printed in China
Orchard Books is a division of Hachette Children's Books, an Hachette UK company.
www.hachette.co.uk

SCOOP
the Digger!

David Wojtowycz

little ORCHARD

Scoop the digger thought that he did
the best job on the building site.

He loved to dig the deepest holes.

DIG! DIG!

He loved to show off
his super-strong arm.
"Look what I can do!"
he boasted.

Tipper the truck went by, carrying a heavy load of sand.

"What an easy job you have!" said Scoop.

"You try it!" replied Tipper, pouring out his sand.

RUMBLE! RUMBLE!

"Okey-dokey," said Scoop.
But he could only pick up
a little bit of sand at a time.

Huff! Puff!

So he had to make fifteen journeys!

Then Hook the crane went by, swinging big planks of wood.

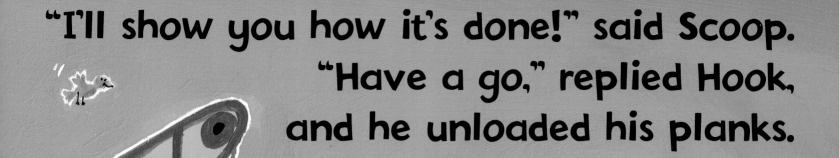

"I'll show you how it's done!" said Scoop.
"Have a go," replied Hook,
and he unloaded his planks.

Klink! Klonk!

"No trouble!" thought Scoop.
But going up and down
the high ramps made
him feel awfully dizzy.

Next, Tumble the cement mixer went by.
"I'll teach you a thing or two!" said Scoop.

"Go ahead," Tumble said, and she emptied out her cement.

splosh! splosh!

"Easy-peasy!" chuckled Scoop.

He tried to lift the cement,
but it was too heavy.

He tried to push the cement,
but it was too runny.

O-oh!

What a mess there was!
Scoop was very tired and
his super-strong arm ached.
But worst of all . . .

. . . he was stuck!

"HELP!" Scoop cried.

whoosh!

Scoop was clear of the cement!

"Thank you!" said Scoop. "And I'm sorry I was bossy. Your jobs aren't easy at all."

"Neither is digging," said Tipper.

"But Scoop, today you were so busy doing our jobs you forgot your own!" smiled Tumble.

They all laughed.

And Scoop couldn't wait to get
back to his favourite job . . .

DIG! DIG!